Fur and Felony

OrangeBooks Publication

1st Floor, Rajhans Arcade, Mall Road, Kohka, Bhilai, Chhattisgarh 490020

Website: www.orangebooks.in

© **Copyright, 2024, Author**

All rights reserved. No part of this book may be reproduced, stored in a retrieval system, or transmitted, in any form by any means, electronic, mechanical, magnetic, optical, chemical, manual, photocopying, recording or otherwise, without the prior written consent of its writer.

First Edition, 2024
ISBN: 978-93-6554-332-2

FUR AND FELONY

AKSHAT VASDEV & ABHAY VASDEV

Orange Books Publication
www.orangebooks.in

Content

Chapter - 1
Ambush 1

Chapter - 2
Terror 4

Chapter - 3
Breaking Point 8

Chapter - 4
On the Edge 11

Chapter - 5
Breakout 13

Chapter - 6
Pursuit 18

Chapter - 7
Realization 22

Chapter - 8
Frenzy 28

Chapter - 9
Tension 40

Chapter - 10
Bloodhound 48

Chapter - 11
　Survival 52

Chapter - 12
　Trail 64

Chapter - 13
　War 75

Chapter - 1
Ambush

My name's Billy. And I'm a rottweiler. Sometimes, things can go from normal to horribly crazy in a matter of seconds. And that's exactly what happened to me and Ron Smith as he was reading a book, and I was lying down next to him chewing a toy absent-mindedly.

It was a fine monday afternoon, and nothing bad had happened yet. It was just Ron and me.

Mary Smith, who is Ron's wife, was at a friend's house in Miami, two hours away from where we were. She is a businesswoman and travels a lot, meaning that it's just Ron and me most of the time, and when she is back she is too tired. So that's why Ron convinced her to take a vacation at her friend's house in Miami.

We didn't really go outside or to dog beaches, but we just stayed home and did practically nothing. I know, dear reader, it was quite boring. But me and my chew toy lived through it. Not to worry.

So, during boredom, I heard a sound that made me jump up and wag my tail. The doorbell! *Ring! Ring!* The person outside must've been angry or just downright busy, but still, it was rude since the guy didn't even give Ron a chance to get up. "Jeez, jeez! I'm coming, I'm coming!"

sighed Ron in exasperation. "I thought the neighbors and I had already resolved this issue..." he grumbled under his breath. I was up, waiting for Ron to open the door, to see who was outside.

When Ron looked out the window, he looked surprised. For obvious reasons. There were two men outside who looked like people who would deliver pizza, but the thing was that Ron had never ordered any. He looked downright confused but then snapped into a smile as he opened the door.

"Delivery to Juan Rodriguez!", said the man outside. The other man was carrying the pizza.

Ron understood. "Oh, I guess you're at the wrong place! My name's Ron, and there's no Juan Rodriguez in this house! Must've been a misunderstanding."

The men looked at each other. "Juan and Ron... must've gotten it wrong. C'mon Aaron, you were supposed to figure the names out!" said one of the men.

Aaron still looked like he knew, what he was doing. "Doesn't matter Luke, at least I got the address right."

Ron chuckled. "Oh no! This address never ordered pizza!" Aaron looked deep into Ron's eyes, and said, "Oh no, I wasn't talking about pizza." Then Aaron delivered a quick jab in between Ron's eyes, and I thought about a million things in that one second.

First, blazing rage. Second, he was the pizza man! I never thought that pizza delivery guys could be dangerous! And third, a sense of protectiveness for Ron. All I wanted to do then was to humble those men and chase them away from Ron. But forget my thoughts- I had to help Ron.

Ron looked dazed, but I jumped at Aaron, without wasting a second. "Oof! Luke, get the dog!" Luke grabbed my neck and tried to pull me away, but I didn't budge as I tried to bite his face off. Luke will not be pulling me away from this scumbag. Not after what he did to Ron.

Luke seemed to give up on pulling me away, but the last thing I saw was his fist as he punched my nose, sending me flying.

Chapter - 2
Terror

I opened my eyes.

And I didn't like what I saw.

Somehow, those two "pizza" men had dragged us two in a dark room, with a desk, a chair, and a lamp. It eerily resembled to a torture room. Wait, uh! Forget that thought. I was muzzled and tied to a metal pole, which didn't budge no matter how hard I struggled. On the chair was Ron, his hands tied behind his back and duct tape on his mouth.

I growled at Aaron and Luke and tried to bark menacingly, but the muzzle was so tight that I couldn't. I tried some more and wiggled around and tried to throw myself towards them, but all those efforts resulted in vain.

It was a very dark room, just like those torture rooms in movies. I was muzzled and leashed onto a pole, which seemed to do nothing when I tugged.

I growled and tried to bark, but sadly, the muzzle wasn't allowing me to even move my mouth.

I didn't give up. I knew it was hopeless to keep throwing myself at those two thugs, but I still had to try. For Ron.

Terror

Aaron and Luke were in the corner of the room, whispering to each other, barely audible. Ron was knocked out, but it looked like a matter of time before he woke up. I looked at the two men. Both seemed to be holding a handgun, which looked loaded. I shivered. I knew what guns could do. I looked around and saw numerous types of weapons, ranging from metal bats to knives. It sure was one scary room, but what I noticed most was the money. Tons of it. It was obvious that the men had kidnapped Ron for Mary's money, but I still wondered what they would do with it. They already had tons of money, and first off, why did they even kidnap me? Maybe because I was a nuisance and was hurting them? Anyway, that wasn't the point. What scared me the most was what they would do to Ron.

It looked like the two men had finally finished their conversation and were looking at both of us. Aaron walked toward Ron with a metal bucket filled with what looked like cold water. Aaron dumped it on Ron causing him to jolt in his chair, shivering.

I growled at both men. This was too much. Ron looked horrible. Beat up, swollen eye, dripping with water, he was saying something through his duct tape, obviously not possible to hear, what he was saying.

Luke came from the corner and loaded his pistol. "You see this, Ron? It's a handgun. Loaded. And look at you! You look horrible, Ron!" Luke exclaimed. "Damn, this is going to be good!" He pointed his gun at Ron's forehead. I started growling and shaking my entire body, desperate to get to Ron. Ron looked petrified, looking at Luke and shaking his head. Aaron tore the duct tape off his mouth, and Ron gasped, taking deep breaths.

"Both of you are PSYCHOS! Stop this! Get me OUT!!!!!" screamed Ron. Luke looked amused, and Aaron looked like he just wanted to get this over with. I had never seen Ron like this before. I growled as loud as I could ever and shook the pole hard. Aaron looked at me with annoyance. "Say Luke, about the dog. Why did we even bring him here?"

"Huh? Oh yeah, the dog! I forgot about him!" He chuckled. "Well, now that he's here we can't do anything about it! Rottweilers are police dogs, and we can't risk a Rotty getting out, now, can we? Also, we could use him." Luke looked at me.

I didn't know what he meant by that, but the most appealing thing to me was he wasn't about to let me go.

Aaron still didn't look satisfied. I kept growling and shaking the pole so badly that I didn't realize that Aaron was in front of me and was going to kick me before it was too late.

POW! I whined and I dropped to the floor as Aaron loomed over me, his face expressionless. "That'll teach you something, you little mutt." I wanted to growl, but my vocal cords decided to not mess with Aaron.

Ron looked at me, his eyes wide with fear, and shouted, "BILLY!" I looked at Ron, still in a daze, blood trickling in my eyes.

Luke looked at both of us and laughed. "All right fellas! That's enough of playtime." Luke turned and stared at Ron. "You know, what I'm about to ask, now, do you?"

Ron looked like he was in despair. We both knew what was coming, Luke stared at Ron, and said, "Where is your wife?"

Chapter - 3
Breaking Point

Ron thought that the guys were crazy. First off, they were asking for money they don't even need since they obviously are already set for life, and second, did they expect him to just give his wife away? I mean, who does that?

I saw at least 10 emotions go through his face in a mere second. Anger, confusion, and hopelessness were only 3 of them. We were at a stalemate. Either we would be tortured until they get the answer, die, or just give them the answer. Ron sure looked hopeless, but he also had a sense of determination on his face. If his wife was in danger, then Ron would help in any way possible.

"Well? What do you say?" Luke lifted his bat and pointed it to Ron's face. I whined in despair, as my consciousness was getting lost due to the hit in the head by stupid Aaron. Jeez, he had a good kick. "You know what will happen if you don't cooperate, don't you?"

Ron looked at Luke, Aaron, me, and back at Luke. I badly wanted to go to Ron's side, but I had my own problems. There was blood in my eyes and my coat was stained red. My eyes were getting blurry, and I was feeling lightheaded and dizzy. Those were not good signs. I felt like, I was about to experience a blackout for the first time in my life.

Luke looked menacingly in Ron's eyes, and so did Aaron as he pointed a loaded gun at Ron.

"NO! Please! Don't shoot me!" Ron pleaded as Aaron took a step forward. "I don't know what to do..." Ron's helpless eyes shot towards me, and I tried to reassure him that everything was going to be right, but I don't think humans understand dog's movements.

"Well, we won't if you just tell us where your wife is. It's simple, really." Luke said as he looked at Aaron. Luke nodded.

Ron looked at Luke looking at Aaron. "Wait, what? Wait, what are you going to do? No, no, please! Give me some-"

BOOM! When a gun goes off in a closed and small room, since it creates a real loud noise, everyone's ears in the room would get hurt, either permanently or temporarily. So that's exactly what happened.

When the gun went off, I had no idea what happened next. I whined loudly, but no one could hear me. Everyone was clutching their ears, but I couldn't. My hearing was 4x better than a human's, so this gun's sound would hurt 4x more. And since I was chained, I couldn't even touch my ears.

My ears ringing, my eyes blurry, I looked up. Ron, Luke, and Aaron were all in a daze. Aaron didn't think this though. But it seemed Ron didn't want to take care of his ears. He was looking at something else. Horrible, tragic, something else.

When I saw it, my eyes went wide with fear. There were only two words going through my head at that point, '*RON'S LEG*'. And I guessed Ron was also thinking the same thing, as his leg had been shot.

Blood was pouring from his leg, and his eyes rolled up in shock. He was in a state of shock and intense pain, as well as blood loss. He had been shot. This was serious.

Luke stopped holding his ears. "JESUS, AARON! You should've thought this through! You thought I wanted to shoot that gun in this dark, small room? IT WAS A STUPID THREAT! You KNOW what happens when you shoot a gun!" Both looked at Ron's leg. Aaron grimaced. "Luke, stop shouting. Look at the positives of the shot. He will have to tell us where she is. And I just found another way we could use the dog." A smile crept up his face. Luke understood. And I did too. If Ron didn't tell them soon, I would be dead.

Chapter - 4
On the Edge

Ron was still knocked out. If he didn't wake up soon, he wouldn't know about my fate. And would not be able to decide what to do. It was a matter of whether he wanted a safe wife or both of us to die. The answer seemed clear, and I already knew what Ron would do. But the actual question was; what's next?

Aaron walked up to injured Ron. "He's not dead." He said, checking his pulse. I sighed much like a dog would. Aaron then went to fill up his bucket with cold water and came back with a fresh bucket of water to dump on Ron's head.

Aaron leaned forward and dumped it. Ron jumped and grimaced as he put pressure on his bad leg. "Ouch! Damn!" Ron tried to clutch his leg but couldn't. "Seriously? You're going to kill me like this!"

Aaron looked at Ron. "Don't worry, you're not going to die. But if you don't tell us-" He pointed the gun at me. "He's the one getting shot."

Ron looked at Aaron in disbelief. "What? No!" He looked even more helpless than before. This was getting out of hand.

Luke looked at Ron. "All you have to do is TELL US." He seemed to be irritated by the way he looked at Ron.

Ron whimpered as Aaron inched near me, making sure I was still at gunpoint. Ron finally gave in. "Fine! But please- don't shoot my dog!" Luke smiled. "Alright! So where is she?"

Ron seemed to be weighing whether to lie or not. He also didn't want to risk it, because if they somehow figured out, he was lying, I would surely be dead.

"M-Miami." Ron muttered.

"Miami, eh? That's like what, a two-hour drive from here? Should be a piece of cake, say, Aaron?"

Aaron lowered his gun. So far, for the two kidnappers, everything was going according to their plan.

"Luke, we don't want to waste time. Get the car ready. We need to go now." Aaron kept his gun in his pocket and opened the door outside. "Hurry up and figure out what to do with them." And he left.

"Well, I guess Aaron gave me a big job! Killing you would not be fun, would it? I guess, hmm. We could just leave you here!" Luke chuckled to himself and left.

I was about to black out when Ron said, "Billy, are you alright? You don't look in good shape." He was worried about me? Look in the mirror! His eyes were determined to get out now, but this was stalemate. We had to get out or starve, but how?

Chapter - 5
Breakout

With Luke and Aaron gone, it was just me and Ron again. Except in a dark room. And no calm feelings. Everything felt tense and jumpy, like Luke would come in again and say, "Surprise! Don't want you getting out, do I?"

Ron scooted the chair toward me and turned sideways, his hands facing me. Ron then tried to pry my muzzle off, but it was no joke. He could barely move his hands. I tried to stand up, but had no success. I tried again, and I stumbled into the wall, but the wall helped me from tripping. So, now that I was up my muzzle touching Ron's hands, it should've been easier to get it off.

Turns out, it wasn't. Ron was touching my muzzle but couldn't get a hold of the straps.

He tried and failed multiple times. In about an hour or so (can't see the time), he finally stuck a finger in my muzzle. It hurt my cheek, since the muzzle was strapped tight, but it was the best he could do. He then pushed the strap back, taking off one of the straps. Two more to go, but I shook the muzzle off with great effort.

Yes! My muzzle! I could bark, growl, bite, and even take off the ropes which tied Ron to the chair! I bit the ropes, and with my sharp canine teeth, the ropes eventually broke open. Ron, with his hands free, took off the ropes which tied his legs to the chair. He winced. His bad leg was still, well, bad, and was going to get worse if he didn't treat it soon. Eventually, Ron stood up and limped over to me, where I was already working on my ropes. I managed to bite off one of the ropes connected to my hands and with Ron's help, I was free and able to walk and run. Ron smiled at me, and said, "Let's get out of here."

I knew not to jump at Ron, since he could fall, so I licked his shin. Ron turned the doorknob, but it was locked.

He looked at me in confusion, but it was obvious. We had underestimated Luke and Aaron. We were trapped.

I looked at Ron, but his eyes were still determined. And then I had an idea. My plan might have been stupid, but I still had to try. And so, I barked as loud as I can. I kept barking for what seemed like forever, so someone could hear me. Ron joined in the act. "Help! We're stuck in this room! Help!!!"

We both were desperate, but we had to do something besides give up and starve. If I had to place my bets, I bet that we were in the middle of the woods, but, since Aaron said something about a car, there had to be roads. Or at least dirt tracks. So that would mean we were somewhere local, but stuck irrespective of whatever we do. Somewhere local in the woods would mean camps, cabins, that kind of a thing. So, either a bunch of scouts would rescue us or some campers. Either way, we would get rescued.

I tried howling with my hollow throat, and man, it was loud. But nothing worked. No matter how hard I howl or bark, nothing worked. Ron wasn't giving up, but it was already dawning on him that nothing would work. He looked at me, but it looked like he wasn't determined anymore. He was scared. Then, his eyes rolled back in his head, and he blacked out.

I sat there waiting for him to come back. He had obviously blacked out due to the wound in his leg and immense pain, but that wasn't the problem. He was the only human here. I couldn't do anything alone, much less find food and water. I relied on Ron for that, but now it wasn't possible. So, even if I somehow found a way to escape, I would need to take Ron with me. But now Ron was knocked out.

I was also trying to think of ways to escape when he came back. Ram the door open? Probably wouldn't work. That stuff only works in the movies and if you're buff, which Ron isn't. Call for help? We already tried that, and much to our surprise, we were stuck and there was no one to help us. My shoulders slumped. Was there any way out? Was Luke and Aaron's plan really going to work?

I looked around and saw the same old stuff. Money, bats, guns. None of that will help. Wait! Bats and guns? I stood up and assessed the amount of ammo and guns we had. It wasn't much, since they probably don't use a lot of guns, but it was enough to bust a hole through the door, and then use a bat to knock it open.

I looked at Ron. He was still knocked out, and I didn't want to do anything till he woke up. So, I sat there pondering. What will we do when we get out? If we really are abandoned in the middle of the forest, how are we going to get out? How do we know Luke and Aaron don't have a bunch of minions guarding us? I mean, that's unlikely, but it is something to think about. There were a lot of questions unanswered, and a very little time. Ron had to wake up quickly. And I had to do something about it.

I remembered how Aaron woke up Ron twice. With water. Cold. I never saw them take the bucket outside with them, so it must've been here somewhere.

I snooped around the chair, table, guns, and money until I saw the bucket at the corner, next to a tap which runs cold water. I turned on the tap with my paw and it started filling up the bucket. I didn't want the bucket too heavy, since my mouth would probably not be able to hold it, but just enough to dump it on Ron.

When I felt the bucket was just right, I held it up with my mouth and walked over to Ron, who was still knocked out. I didn't want to drop the bucket straight up on Ron, since that will hurt, so I kept it next to him and tipped it over with my paw, and the cold water spilled everywhere.

Ron jerked up and grimaced, as his leg started hurting again. "Woah! Ouch, ouch, ouch! Billy? You woke me up!" He grinned. "Although that still doesn't feel good."

I then trotted over to the guns and bats. It seemed Ron understood as he looked through them. "Huh! We could use that to get out. Alright, here goes," as he stood up, grabbing a gun. "Never used this before, but let's try."

He had some trouble trying to load the gun, since he had never done that, but once it was loaded, he covered his ears. I also covered mine. "Alright, here goes nothing," I heard him say, and the gun exploded with bullets hitting the door with tons of force. Ron was having trouble with just keeping the gun under control, but all the bullets were still hitting the door. Then the gun steamed, and it was out of ammo.

He then grabbed a bat and whacked the door repeatedly hard. The sound was deafening for me. The holes made from the gun helped, as the bat decimated the door, creating huge holes, I could jump through. Then, Ron put his hand through the door and touched the doorknob, twisting it, and the door opened.

We escaped.

Chapter - 6
Pursuit

The question was: now what? I had been right about us in the middle of the woods, with no one to help us. I wondered how they had managed to set up such an effective environment for kidnapping. They had tons of resources, as well as weapons. But we had those too.

Ron looked at his bat, which was completely fine. He then dropped the gun and limped inside to get a handgun. "We'll probably need this," he said. He put it in his pocket and together we walked deeper into the forest.

There was a strap on the bat, which you could use to sling over your shoulder, so that's what he did. He looked armed for the battle, but I knew Ron. Even if he brought a million weapons, he has a big heart. I doubt he would even use this stuff anytime.

We trudged along the path the car that Aaron and Luke had used to drive away, as it was our best chance of escaping. There was light rain, with a calm patter as the water on the leaves dripped onto us and around us. I just wanted to forget everything that had happened. Ron getting shot, Mary going to get kidnapped and stolen from, and two thugs who have guns, money, and bats. This was completely horrifying.

I knew we would have to go to Miami to stop them. They were going to hurt Mary and her friends, and Ron and I did not want that to happen at any cost. We would feel guilty, and we would be completely strapped for money especially since Ron's job, doesn't pay us much at all.

We obviously needed Mary, not only because we loved her, but also because we wouldn't be able to live this life without her. She had been supplying us with things, we needed for so long and we never took a moment to appreciate it. But as always, at the time of crisis, we remember to appreciate things. That's how it always works, regardless of what the situation is.

Logically, Aaron and Luke were not dumb. They weren't going to just put us near the highway or near any type of help. We were most likely deep in the woods, and they must've had help paving this road. From someone else. Two people will obviously not be able to do it, and they probably used a bulldozer or something. This place could've been a construction site back in the day. They would've had permission from someone else to do all this. After all, bulldozers and huge things attract attention and authorities, so they must've had permission from someone.

Looking at it this way, whoever kidnapped us is not just Aaron and Luke. No, two people could've kidnapped us and done all that. There had to be someone else. Someone much more powerful than Luke and Aaron.

This was just getting worse and worse, and I started wondering how Mary might have been.

I was having fun. Lots of fun.

It was a good thing Ron sent me to Miami with my friends, because I knew, I needed a break anyways. I had been working for countless hours every day, and Ron finally convinced me to go and take a break. It was worth it.

I had invested in a stock, and that it unexpectedly plummeted. After that, not only did I lose my money, but so did all my clients. It was horrifying, embarrassing, and I was guilty. That's why Ron convinced me to take a break. I needed one. I had so much stress on my shoulders, and this vacation was taking it away. Thank God.

I was lying down in my hotel bed. It was calm here, and it gave me space to think about what to do after I got back home. I needed to take care of this investment issue quickly, and I don't think a week vacation will really affect our situation, although I was aware of losing time.

I really had to get my mind off this. The deeper I thought about it, the more stress built up.

I snapped out of my thoughts as the phone rang. I reached for it, expecting my friends to call me over for a party.

I held the phone in my ear. "Hello," I said, "This is Mary. Who is this?" I was startled when I heard a ragged, but familiar voice. It was Ron! "H-Hey Mary. Are you alright?"

I was shocked at his voice. He had been hurt, or worse. "Yes, I'm doing fine. Are you hurt? Your voice is ragged. What happened?"

Ron sighed over the phone. "Lots of things happened Mary. Where should I even start? Anyways, we don't have time. I'll give you a quick summary of what happened, and I'm coming to you right now. It's urgent."

As I was listening to the story, my eyes just kept on getting wider and wider, and my voice speechless. "Luke and Aaron," I whispered to myself.

"Are they there yet? They should be halfway there. Be safe, please. Tell the hotel staff and your friends about this. You need to be safe at all cost. I'm coming. Please. Don't-" His voice cracked like he was about to cry. "Just be safe. Please. These guys are dangerous."

I was shocked at the news. Luke and Aaron. I managed to mutter, "Don't worry. Take care of yourself," and hung up the phone. Luke and Aaron. Luke and Aaron. I remembered them, oh yes. They were one of my clients, and it seems they're plotting revenge on me for my invested money. They want the money back at all cost.

Chapter - 7
Realization

I looked at Aaron in surprise. "you're saying all this is my fault?! What's gotten into your mind, Aaron?!"

Aaron looked at me. We were driving to Miami, now that we knew where Mary was. She ruined everything.

Aaron raised his eyes. "No, no, this is your fault. You were the one who presented the idea of stealing Santiago's black money! You were the one who told me to give the black money to Mary, so that she can help us investment it without knowing! I just did the work! You were the brains, the mastermind behind all this chaos!"

I sighed. Arguing with Aaron was never good, since his big ego would never allow him to accept, he was wrong.

I looked at the highway. This was a long ride, and we still had miles to go. "You could have easily disagreed with my plan, or at least explained to me that I was being stupid. I was just desperate for money, and you knew that."

"You know what? Let's shut down this stupid argument. There's no point in arguing either way. We must think. You know Santiago is going to kill both of us, if we don't get his money back. He's still running his drug business, but we got kicked out. We need to get back in, otherwise we'll just be some random homeless people begging for spare change." Aaron sighed and put his head down in his hands. "Give me a moment, Luke. Give me a moment."

I understood. We had to steal Mary's money to give to Santiago Delgado otherwise, we would die for sure. Santiago wasn't the type of guy who spared people, who stole his money.

Aaron finally looked up. "I know what to do. But this is desperate, and you know desperate plans don't always work." He glared at me.

"Ok, ok. Just tell me what your plan is."

"Here goes." He sighed. "You won't like it. We need to call Santiago now. We need to reason with him and tell him we were going to get the money back, because I believe he already knows that we might have stolen his drug money." He stressed the word might. "We will tell him about Ron and the dog, and some of his guys will go and check on them. You know for a fact that if they escaped, they would be chasing us. If they somehow escaped, then Santiago's guys will kill him. Hopefully."

He had a point there. That room which we left Ron and the dog in, was one of many rooms hidden in forests. Each room was stacked with guns and melee weapons, as well as money, if needed. If Ron and the dog got each other out of the ropes, then they could easily use the guns and weapons to destroy the door, knocking it down.

"It's worth a try," I said, picking up my phone and handing it to Aaron. "Call him. If we don't want to die, call him."

"Yes, hello. Who is this?"

I looked at Luke. Luke nodded with reassurance, but it wasn't reassuring. "This is Aaron. I'm sitting with Luke. I need you to go tell Mr. Delgado about, what I'm about to say. He needs to know about this."

I told him the whole story of us as pizza men kidnapping Ron and a dog and figuring out where Mary was. I told the guy I was talking to, that we were going to give Santiago his money, but he'll have to wait. I told him to ask Santiago to check the room, and then chase Ron down if he escaped.

He said he'll convey the message to Santiago, and then hung up. I told Luke what happened. He nodded. "They shouldn't have escaped unless they got through the ropes. We checked thoroughly and there was nothing to worry about on them. They cannot get out."

"Yeah. Phew. I hope Santiago doesn't kill us. I bet he already knows; we were the ones who stole the money or at least helped someone else steal the money. We were the ones who were guarding the safes that day after all." I sighed. "This is going to be one long day."

I opened the door and tried to find my friends. At last, I called them. "Hey, Mary, where are you? We're at the lobby of the hotel, waiting for you!"

"I'm in my room. Listen, I need to talk to you all about something. Put the phone on speaker," I said.

I narrated the entire story to my friends and told them they also need to talk to the hotel staff. Her friends agreed. "We'll keep you safe in this hotel. I don't think anywhere else is safer, since we're on the top floor of this hotel and it'll take some time for them to figure out where you are. Don't worry Mary. We aren't going anywhere."

She hung up. They had also told me to stay in my room and relax. So, I did and thought about what was bound to happen next.

I was thinking about how they got so much money in the first place to give me so that I could invest. Did they do something illegal? Did they borrow money from others? They didn't win the lottery or anything like that which would give tons of money, but they also weren't the type of guys to beg. I mean, I knew Luke well, since he was easy-going and friendly, and I knew Aaron was the type of guy to have work first and fun later. Fun was the last thing on his mind, for god's sake. But I never would've thought, that they were the type of guys who would team up, kidnap, and steal.

There was something fishy going on here which I didn't know about. I should call Ron and ask him what he knows.

I picked up the phone and dialed Ron's number. He immediately picked up. "Hey, Mary, what happened? Are you alright?"

"Yes, I'm fine. I told my friends and the hotel staff about what's happening. They're keeping me safe. They haven't come yet. And there's something I want to tell you. Luke and Aaron used to be my clients, and when the investment went down, they left the job, and since they were the ones who gave me the money, they're coming to get it back. And I think they did something illegal to get the money."

"Do you think they're part of a drug business? Because when they kidnapped me, they had tons of money in that one room. Guns, bats, traps and what not. And we only escaped from the forest because of Billy and the paved road which Luke and Aaron used to commute to the forest. They could've only done that with huge machines of some kind. They must've had permission, and if they are part of the drug business, their boss has a lot of power. But you also would agree that their being in the drug business is a possibility, and we don't have any clue."

"It's the most likely possibility. But that would mean that it's not just Luke and Aaron. I bet their boss is mad at them for having stolen his money, so either he's going to help Luke and Aaron get his money back, or he's going to kill both of them." I shuddered. "Thinking about it is scary."

"Yeah, I could just wonder how it is for you. You're the one who's being targeted. But don't worry, I'm coming."

"Yeah, right. What are you going to do?" I laughed. "Alright Ron, take care of yourself. Be safe."

"You be safe. I'm going to be calling frequently, alright? 5 more minutes and I'll call again. Please be safe." And he hung up.

I sighed. I couldn't do anything. All I could do was wait for them to come. With some other people. Probably not.

So many questions unanswered, I was left vulnerable. Just waiting for chaos and I could do nothing to stop it.

Chapter - 8
Frenzy

The phone finally rang, and I let Aaron grab it. Santiago's men were about to let us know if Ron and the dog escaped and if they were going to help kidnap Mary if Ron hadn't escaped.

Aaron held the phone up to his ear. "This is Aaron."

"Hello, Aaron. It seems that your guys, Ron and the dog, have escaped."

I looked at Aaron and he looked at me, his eyes wide. "Sorry, what? Can you explain what the place looks like?"

"Empty gun shells. Tons. You're bad at this stuff." He chuckled over the phone. Aaron growled. "Just tell me what to do. We don't have time," Aaron said.

"Alright, alright. Stop by the nearest gas station. Stall there. A car will come up and you will all go to Mary's hotel. Another car will go to Ron right now to stop them. Send us the location of your gas station."

"Alright." He held the phone away from his ear. "Oi, Luke. Turn around. The gas station is right there." I took a U-turn and took a lane near the gas pumps. "I'll fill up the gas," I said, and turned off the engine. I grabbed the gas pump and started filling up the gas. Aaron was still talking to the man on the phone, as I put the gas pump away and started the engine. I turned around and parked at the parking space.

"Well, all we could do is wait," I told Aaron. Santiago's men were ruthless, and I knew Santiago. He would do anything for money, even help traitors, like Luke and Aaron themselves.

We waited for a long time. After about a little more than an hour, a car parked right next to us and out came four men. Aaron opened the door to step out and meet them. I walked out of the car too and faced the men.

"Howdy there," I said. "What took you so long?"

"We were busy. That's all you need to know," He added, as I cocked an eyebrow. "Let's take a move on. We need to get to Mary quickly. If Ron escaped, then he would've called Mary. I think Mary remembers who you are. She already told some people about this." The man opened the door to his car and sat down. "Here's the deal. You lead the way. I'll be behind you." He motioned for the other 3 men to sit down in his car.

Me and Aaron sat down in our car, Aaron on the steering wheel. "See you at the hotel," I told the man, and closed the door.

Aaron started the engine, and we took off. We only had about 30 minutes left till we reached Mary's hotel. I picked up the phone and mindlessly scrolled through my messages to try to get my mind off this "mission" for black money. But it was impossible for me to relax. I was tensed, stressed, and nervous all at the same time. What if we don't get the money? Me and Aaron would be screwed. Santiago's men will chase us down and probably kill us. There was a lot at risk here. But looking at it that way, what is not risky?

I looked up from the phone. The sky was clear, with barely any clouds. The sun was shining, and the mood was supposed to be great. Who wouldn't try to go to the beach right now? It was perfect. But we had a drug lord on our tail, if we didn't get his money, 4 men behind our car to make sure we don't make a run for it, and our previous boss with black money, she never knew about. This was complicated. But at the end, the skies were still clear, and the children were still playing. How careless. Sometimes I envy children. They have so much time to do, whatever they want and get whatever they want to get. I wonder if I used to be like a careless child. After all, I never anticipated that my career would be with psychotic drug lords. But that's another story.

I sighed and put my head down to my knees. "I need to sleep. That's probably the only way I could get my mind off this horrendous situation." Aaron nodded. "I don't care if you sleep or not, just make sure you're not drowsy when you wake up. We'll need all the adrenaline and energy we can get." I nodded and put my head on the headrest. How comfortable. The noise of the tyres of the car on the road made it even better. I closed my eyes and sighed in exhaustion. But no matter how hard I tried; I couldn't sleep well. It was a good rest for my eyes, but no sleep. My leg muscles were ready to jump and my arms ready to shoot. Why, oh why was my mind like this? I didn't want to be jumpy and ready to fight. Ugh! Stupid body.

I opened my eyes. Five minutes had passed. Only five. At least Aaron had something to do, like drive. I was just sitting there and doing nothing besides thinking about how things could go wrong. If Mary is on the upper floor, and the hotel staff figures out something wrong, then we're screwed. We would be trapped, and no matter how much I think about it, we're screwed in every way. We would be arrested, and then what? Interrogated? Then they would figure out about our money. Then we would be sentenced to jail for a long time. After all, drugs are taken seriously.

Jeez. We were screwed either way.

And how were we supposed to pass by security anyways? Will we split up into small groups and figure out what happens next?

Then the phone rang. It was probably from the guys behind us. I picked up the phone and held it up to my ear. "Hello, this is Luke speaking. What is it?"

"Hey, Luke. We're the guys you met earlier at the gas station."

"Yeah, I remember. What happened? Why'd you call?"

"I see police. 2 cars. And I don't really know better, but I think they're on our tail. My guys have been noticing the police following us, but not right behind us. They're two cars away from us, but I don't think the two cars between us would also be smuggling anything. I think the guy you kidnapped had called the police on us."

"But how would he know what our cars look like?"

"That's what I don't know. But I'm guessing the police have been tracking us."

"With what?"

"Isn't it obvious? Our phones."

I groaned. Their phones were their only source of communication with everyone they knew, including each other. Aaron seemed to have picked up the conversation.

"Well, what now? They know that we're in this car, so it won't really help to throw the phones out the window, right?"

"Yeah, exactly," the man said through the phone. "That's the problem. And these police officers have been on our tail for 10 minutes. Any moment now, and they'll do something to get us."

"Well, what do we do?"

"I'm thinking we run for our lives."

"Alright. We need to get out of the highway though. There's too much room for the police to chase us, and our cars are not as fast as the police's. We need to get to an exit ASAP."

"Understood."

"Start speeding up when I do. We need to split up. You take the next exit, and Aaron and I will take the next."

"This'll be risky, but we got to take the risk. Good luck." And with that, he disconnected.

I looked ahead. There wasn't much traffic, and they weren't in as much danger as we were in. In the highway, the police can easily catch up with us, that meaning we needed to pick up full speed.

Still thinking, I heard a loud siren interrupt my thoughts. "Aaron! Speed up!"

Aaron's leg floored the accelerator, and we took off. I didn't dare look back, but I hoped the men in the car also sped up. "Keep going! Don't take your foot off the accelerator."

The car was whizzing past the highway at a blinding pace, the other cars could not match with the speed of our car. I tried looking back but couldn't see anything due to our speed. The fact that we were still picking up pace bothered me.

I still heard sirens behind us. By now, the other men should have gotten away... but I still saw their car through my window mirror.

I was confused. *What?* They should've left by now! Aaron's and my exit was just around the corner at this point, and their exit had long gone.

Damn it! Maybe the police cut them off and they had no choice but to follow us. *We might be screwed*, I realized.

Our car was still moving at a blinding pace, just then I saw the exit we were looking for. "Aaron! Get to that exit!" I pointed at it wildly.

He didn't reply, but he dodged cars and swerved between lanes. We barely made it.

I looked behind and still saw the police on our tail. It kind of made sense, since they had sirens and cars would move out of the way. I had no idea where the men were, until I saw their car enter the exit. That was bad. The police car behind me can easily stop the men's car.

They seemed to realize that when they literally went off the road and into a construction site. The car bounced on some rocks and quickly got back onto the road, ramming the police car in accident.

The police car swerved and went completely sideways, flipping upside down. There was another police car behind that one which I couldn't see due to my blocked view.

The men's car was fine except for huge scratches on the side of their car and one broken window. Not good.

Over here, there were cars everywhere unlike the highway with a ton of free space, so it must've been hard for Aaron to drive with the cars, but the cars seemed to be getting out of the way, which was good for us in a way.

I looked back and noticed that the police were catching up with us. I looked at Aaron and was starting to tell him to speed up, but he looked like he was in bad condition. He was sweating a lot, and his muscles seemed to be working overtime, which was bad. It looked like he was cramping up, but he wasn't stopping which was the good part. But I had a bad feeling he would stop any moment now.

Aaron for some reason pushed his phone to me. "Call. Santiago," he said.

I looked at him in disbelief. "Santiago? What- why him? He would literally kill us, you know!"

"It's our only chance. And you know it. He can either help us or kill us. I think it's worth it." He was breathing hard now.

I looked at his face for any emotion but didn't see anything. "Hmm. Alright, fine. But if we die, that's on you."

He didn't reply. I nervously dialed the cartel's number. Was this our only chance? My mind scanned for more choices, but it was completely blank. Either we get arrested for a very long time, or we get help from Santiago. Or else we die.

The phone rang once, and somebody in Santi's mansion picked up. "And who the hell are you?" The man from the other side had a gruff and deep voice.

I gulped. I remembered him. He was the right-hand man of Santiago. Why did he pick up the phone, of all people?

"Hello. This is Luke and Aaron. We're in deep trouble right now, and we need your help." The last sentence was more like a question.

"Luke and Aaron, eh? The men who stole Santi's money? You really think we're just going to let you go like that?"

I looked at Aaron in desperation, but he had his eyes on the road. "We're the only ones who know where Mary is. We're being chased by the cops right now. That's why we need your help. Without us, Santi isn't going to get his money back."

"Oh really? What if you just tell me where Mary is right now, and you two won't be the only ones who know? How about it? Get arrested, or tell me?"

"I won't tell you even if I was at gunpoint. And you know his money's screwed unless I tell you, which I won't. So, it's either to save the only people who can get Santi's money back or let them get arrested and he won't be getting his money back. Ever."

That seemed to shut him up. I took the phone from my ear and exhaled, shocked that I was talking to the second-in-command of this infamous drug cartel like that. Yep, we're screwed for sure now.

I put the phone back on my ear. He seemed to be reconsidering sending help. "Fine. I'll send help. You just do whatever you need to do and we're going to send help. Probably shoot them down." He declined before I even had a chance to speak.

"I think we're good." I told Aaron. He didn't say anything.

The police were catching up on us quickly, but I didn't want to pressurize Aaron. He already had a lot of pressure.

In no time, the police were just next to us. The policeman was looking straight at me. I gulped.

I grabbed my gun and tried to hide it from the officer, but he saw it. He pulled out his gun and aimed it directly at me. *Can he even do that legally? I don't think officers can shoot unless shot at...*

I didn't want to pull out my gun since then the officer has the right to shoot us down. But the man's voice rang in my ears... *probably shoot them down.*

Pretty stupid advice. So, I didn't.

The officer seemed to be grabbing something like a loudspeaker. *GET OUT OF THE CAR NOW, OTHERWISE YOU WILL BE ARRESTED!* The man said on the loudspeaker.

Aaron kept on driving, but I knew he had heard that loudspeaker, since it was so loud. The police car sped up until it was in front of us. Bad.

"Aaron! Hit the brakes!" Aaron thankfully understood. As soon as the car went ahead of us, thinking we would hit it, Aaron hit the brakes slowly, making sure we didn't flip over.

Our car reversed unexpectedly, but I think the men behind us were caught. I heard a loud bump and a hiss as we crashed into their car.

I quickly opened the door and stepped out, looking at what happened. The men were stepping out and looking at their car in shock. Its engine was smoking.

"How?" I whispered to myself. I snapped back to reality as a man shook me. "We need to get the hell out of here. I'm going in the trunk."

"GUYS! HURRY UP!" Aaron shouted, pointing to the policemen getting out of the car and pointing tasers at the three other men. The man who said he was going in the trunk was already in. I put my hands up, but in about a second, I was inside the car. "GET IN THE TRUNK!" I shouted to the men, closing my door. Aaron started the engine and hesitantly sped up. I heard the thumping of the men getting inside. I looked back to the horror of the policemen using tasers on the men. One man got his gun out and shot the policeman, but the other policeman shot him. "There's one in the trunk!" The officer said.

I grabbed my gun and opened the window, pointing at the policeman. I was about to fire when the officer shot my gun out of my hand. "WOAH!" I looked at my hands, bleeding as the bullet had skimmed them.

Aaron sped up, but the officer was literally holding on to the trunk and was on top of the car. The officer opened the trunk, to the surprise of the man pointing up a gun at him.

Yes! I thought. *Get him!*

The man in the trunk shot the police officer once, and then again, but missed. The officer groaned and almost slipped off, holding on to the trunk handle for his dear life. He then shot the man in the trunk once and fell off the car, rolling on the road.

I heard a scream in the back of the trunk and loud groaning. "Oi! Are you good back there? Where'd you get shot?" I attempted to climb to the back but was unsuccessful.

"I got shot; I got shot." He was mumbling.

"Where?"

"I-I don't know!!"

"Can you call Santiago?"

"Santiago?" He sounded confused. Santiago's men were not here yet and they should've been. The police were still on our tail, and somebody had to call Santiago while I shot the crap out of the police.

"Yes! He's our only chance! Otherwise, we get arrested!"

"Oh. Alright. I need a phone." He coughed and groaned.

I looked back at him. "What's your name?"

"Alejandro."

"Alright, Alejandro, call Santiago as soon as possible. I'm just going to get busy for a moment."

Alejandro caught my phone. "Busy?"

I grabbed the gun and opened the window. Aaron looked at me in confusion. "What the hell are you doing?"

"Wait and watch," I said, grinning.

Chapter - 9
Tension

How long? Ron was thinking about the same thing, as he asked the driver how long it would take to reach the hotel. The driver said 15 minutes. Jeez! This trip was longer than I expected. I looked out the window and watched countless cars zooming by on the highway. I then looked at Ron nervously biting his nails and looking out of the window blankly. Ron had called Mary at least 5 times by then, and Mary kept saying the same thing. "Don't worry, Ron. I'll be fine. They aren't here yet." These short talks kept happening after every 10 minutes, and I knew Ron was worried. Who wouldn't? I was also worried sick.

I also couldn't just wait. I had to do something. I had been chewing on my chew toy until it ripped apart at this point. I needed a new toy, and I wasn't about to eat the entire toy and swallow it. I'm not that type of guy.

Ron pulled out his phone again and tapped Mary's number. After 1 ring, she picked up.

"Ron, they aren't here. How are you doing?"

"Just holding on," Ron said. "10 minutes till I come to you. Those bastards must've got caught by the police at this point." Ron sighed. "I called the police, and they said they will try. But, Mary, don't get your hopes high. Either they're injured or have gotten arrested. Let's hope for the best."

"Yeah."

"Alright, Mary. Stay safe."

"Yeah."

"Bye."

And he disconnected the call.

Ron then peered over the seat and looked at the ETA on the driver's GPS. 5 minutes. Better get ready.

I had my eyes stuck on the road. I was sweating like crazy and zigzagging to the best of my ability.

When Luke got the gun, I knew what he was going to do. He was obviously going to put up a fight with the police, but it was no use. With three cars behind us, and a helicopter, shooting anything won't change anything. Santiago's men were close by, yes, but any moment now and we're screwed. Luke started shooting like crazy at tyres, windows, and everything in his vicinity. Nothing happened. The tyres, with some sort of protection on them, kept them from deflating. The windows were bulletproof. Luke's efforts were futile.

It was a miracle that our car hadn't been destroyed yet. I was wondering how we were going to hold up. This car could only take a few more shots, and then it might go down.

I turned the car right. "GUYS! Mary's hotel is RIGHT THERE!" And there it was. A huge hotel you could see from a distance. It had many windows coverings the building, and with its black, sleek, luxurious design from outside, why the rich would not want to go there? Like Mary.

"Keep going!" Alejandro shouted at me. "Any moment now, and Santiago's people will show up! They're not too far!"

I tried nodding but couldn't. All my muscles were working hard and overtime, and I had cramps in my legs and one on my arm. It was hurting a lot, so I decided to take deep breaths and calm down.

It didn't work but at least I tried. I exhaled loudly and shook my head vigorously. I was sweating, cramping, and panicking. It was horrid.

The police cars were still chasing us, trying to get to us before anything bad happened like a car crash. And no, they weren't behind us. They were literally beside us, at the same speed this car was running.

I looked at them and they were looking at me, saying something in their radios. The officer I was looking at nodded, and pulled out his gun, sliding the window open and aiming.

"DUCK!!" I screamed. *BOOM!* A gunshot echoed and I heard a loud groan. I quickly pulled my head up to see that no one was injured, but I saw Luke holding a gun up, which was aimed at the officer I was looking at. I swiveled my head to the officer, and he was groaning in pain loudly, clutching his bloody arm.

Luke looked at me with wide eyes. "DRIVE!!!"

I braked suddenly, and the police cars were not expecting it, and with their momentum, they sped ahead. I looked around and saw an exit, and turning, I merged into the lane. People were obviously freaking out because of the police cars, gunshots, and whatnot, but I didn't care. I turned left slightly, and the car climbed up onto the grass.

I then turned right on the grass and once again, merged into the lane, nearly crashing into a person. I then stepped on to the accelerator, and we sped off, dodging multiple cars. I was sweating like crazy now, since I didn't want to hurt anyone or anything. I decided to stop at a gas station, and I parked there.

"Whoo!" I slumped back in my seat and sighed. I turned on the AC at max. "This is going to be a five-second break." I signaled for Luke to drive. "We got to go." I stepped out of the car.

"Wait! Look at that." Luke pointed at the road, and sure enough, two SUVs showed up, and turned to the gas station. "I guess we're meeting at a gas station again."

Luke got out of the car. The two SUVs parked beside us. One man stepped out. I looked at him. "How's Santiago?"

He shrugged off what I said as if I hadn't said anything. "You should take this car. That car of yours is useless. It'll last 15 minutes, max."

He handed me the keys. "The guns are in the trunk. We'll get Alejandro."

I nodded and handed the keys to Luke. "I'm done driving for a while. You drive."

We sat down and looked at Alejandro getting carried to the other car, leaving our car in the dust. "They would've figured out by now. Luke, leave your phone."

"Huh? Why?" He spoke.

"The only reason they knew we were here was because of our phones. If we leave them here, they will think we're here, but we won't be."

"Huh." He put his phone on the roof of our old, beaten-up car. "Looks like we won't need that."

He turned on the engine and I sat back and relaxed, putting my legs up on the dashboard. I turned on the GPS, but really, there was no need. The hotel was right there.

I jumped out of the car, Ron leashing me. The hotel was huge, and I could only hope Mary was somewhere, up there. We walked in and were stunned by how beautiful the place was.

Four chandeliers lit up the place, lined up perfectly, but really, we didn't need it. We had a perfect view of the sun setting behind the seas, and the waves calmly crashing against the shore. It was a stunning sight.

Tension

I looked around and didn't see Mary around. She must've been somewhere in the hotel, and some people might have been hopefully guarding her.

We went to the front desk and Ron talked to the lady, asking where a lady named Mary was.

"Hello, welcome to the Grand Azure Hotel! How can I help you?"

"Well, you see, I need to find a lady named Mary Smith."

The front desk woman's face suddenly turned serious. "And why exactly do you want to meet a lady named Mary Smith?"

"I'm her husband. I'm here to check on her to make sure she's okay. I'm Ron Smith."

She seemed to believe him. "Well, Mary did tell me of Ron Smith who's her husband. She went to the bar a while ago. I didn't see her leave or anything. I was looking, I swear."

"Thank you! Where is the bar?"

"Just take a left over there, and then you'll see a door. Open it, and you have the bar."

"Thank you so much!" He tugged on my leash and we both walked away and followed the directions she mentioned.

We walked in the bar, and a wave of smell overwhelmed me. I stopped for a moment, but Ron tugged on my leash and whispered, "Come on."

We saw men and women laughing, talking and drinking in peace, but no Mary. Ron looked confused. "The front desk woman mentioned she would be here, and she said she never left, so what happened?" I could tell he was worried. *She might be in the bathroom. I heard drinks can make people puke,* I thought, reassuring myself Mary was alright. I mean, the front desk lady seemed honest. But what if Mary got kidnapped but she never saw it happen? It is a possibility, after all. But let's not think negatively.

I tugged on the leash, looking at the bathroom, hoping Ron could understand that she might be there. He took the hint. We walked in the bathroom normally, but instead of the men's bathroom, we went in the women's bath. Women gave us nasty glares, telling us to get the hell out. But we weren't about to.

"Mary? Are you here?" Ron looked at every woman and seemed more and more discouraged after every glance. One woman walked up to Ron and even said, "Wrong bathroom."

I heard Ron groan quietly. We both left the bathroom and headed over to the front desk lady, who was talking to a couple.

Ron skipped the line and went up to the lady. The couple seemed to be taken aback. "She's not there. She isn't there!" Ron said, pacing back and forth.

"She isn't? Are you sure?"

"I would know if Mary was there! I would see her, but she just wasn't there!"

"She might be back up in her room," the lady said, dialing a number on her telephone. "I'm calling her room right now."

Ron nodded and stepped back. But the lady's telephone never got answered back.

Ron looked in despair and asked the lady where she might be. "I'm wanting to help, but I really can't. I have no idea where she went. And this officer here is telling me you must go to the hospital."

"What? Why?"

The policeman standing next to the lady the entire time walked up to us and whispered, "Because of your shot leg."

Ron looked at him in shock. "What? How do you know that I got shot?"

"Come with me." Ron and the man started walking towards the exit. "You have a bad limp and I see specks of blood on your pant."

Ron looked down. It was true. There were some specks of blood, but not that serious to notice anything. "You rest here. I'll call an ambulance."

I laid down next to Ron. Was he going to have a surgery? And where was Mary?

Chapter - 10
Bloodhound

Aaron sat beside me as I drove our car to our next destination, a gas station. We parked our car in the parking lot, grabbed the keys, and went inside the small store. "Oi, Aaron get that right here", I cocked my head towards the knife. Aaron looked at it and perked his eyebrow. "You sure?" he said. "You never know, when we might need it," I replied. He picked up the knife and went to another aisle. "Alright, you need gum as well?", he questioned me. "Sure", I said. We then scavenged the store hoping to get some grocery which could possibly help us survive. We were about to leave when Aaron walked towards me and said, "Look outside, they're here". I shivered, "Santi's here?". Aaron nodded. "Let's go to the back of the station and out into the woods", he replied, looking scared. "But what about her?", I questioned. "Forget about her, we need to get the heck out of here. We need to tell Santi that Mary's in the trunk.". That's when I noticed the shopkeeper.

He was looking directly at us, shuffling his hands in a drawer. He then fumbled with something black, something familiar. "Ah sh-", *BOOM!* We ducked right in time behind a table. "Oi, Aaron you alright?", I asked, shivering.

"We need to get out of here right now!" Aaron whispered. The shopkeeper grouped up with Santiago's men. *He's working for them,* I thought. *But how did they know we're here?* "They're in there hermano!", he yelled. Thats when he came up, Santiago. "Aaron! Luke! Do not put a show right now! I need to know if you got the money, so I won't have to cut you up that way." He flashed his knife and grinned, knowing we were looking at him. "He's lying", I whispered to Aaron. "Santi! The woman you're looking for is in the trunk! SHE HAS THE MONEY!", I yelled back. Santiago motioned for two men armed with rifles to open the trunk. They lifted the lid up and she was not there. "What the heck?", I murmured. That's when Santiago laughed and pulled out his pistol, "Lying is not a viable option LUKE!".

The shopkeeper pointed at the aisle, we were hiding behind, and shouted, "THEY'RE THERE!" I looked at Aaron and shouted, "RUN!", as Santiago shot the first bullet, the sound reverberating in the shop.

"Aah!" The sound was deafening, but there was no time to stop. We sprinted towards a door, little realizing that it said storage room, when we got closer to it. Aaron tried opening it, but no luck. We both practically jumped when we heard more pistols going off in different directions. They didn't know where we were!

I heard Santiago shouting over the gunshots. "SPREAD APART! GET THEM!" I heard the pounding of footsteps as many people ran in different directions to find us, wherever we were. So far, nobody had. But the shop was small, and this wasn't exactly our lucky day. Mary had somehow escaped, leaving us two with no chance of redemption of getting back in business. Now what?

I flinched as a man with a gun looked at us, abruptly stopping and turning to shoot us down. I was stunned, but Aaron recovered more quickly. He pushed the aisle down to crush the man. The man groaned, and said something like, "They're here..."

With the aisle down, we had no place to hide. We immediately sprinted for our lives to the windows, jumping at the last moment and bracing ourselves for impact. The glass shattered easily when Aaron and I rammed into it. The not so good news was that when we jumped through the window, we didn't land on our feet but on our backs, giving the men time to get to us. I quickly pulled out my gun and shot randomly at multiple people, not hitting a single target. Aaron and I scrambled to our feet and ran to the woods with Santiago right behind us like bloodhounds. "They're catching up on us", I gasped. Aaron looked at me replying, "Nah really?".

We swerved to the right trying to catch them off guard, but it didn't work. "We might have to split up!", Aaron yelled. "It might work, but we might lose each other!", I answered.

Santiago's men were catching up on us, and in a few seconds, they would be on us. We tried gaining speed, but it was no use since we were already exhausted. "Over there!", I yelled. Aaron and I slid under a dead log catching Santiago's men off-guard.

"I DO NOT CARE IF THEY'RE ALIVE, TAKE 'EM DOWN!", Santiago yelled in anger. Bullets zipped around us. I knew this would not end well if it kept going like this, so I pulled out my gun to retaliate. I loaded in some bullets and started firing back, until a bullet struck my stomach; impaling me through the back. I tripped and rolled off a slope, crashing into Aaron and pulling him over into the river. "Luke, what are you doing!", Aaron screamed. I could not think properly, I was bleeding horribly, and my vision was blurring. We were spiraling down the cliff breath-takingly fast, vines grabbing onto us, scarring us. Were we about to die?

The river was moving at an enormous speed. I tried grabbing onto multiple rocks and anything that came in my way. I lost sight of Aaron through the chaos. *At this rate I would drown,* I thought. "Where did they go?!", Santiago yelled up the cliff; at least we got rid of them, I murmured. Thats when I had a burning sensation in my stomach. I started sinking in the water, my vision blurring. I groaned in pain due to the injury I received from the bullet. I tried floating on the water, but it was pointless since I noticed a waterfall ahead of me, "Oh sh-", I gasped.

Chapter - 11
Survival

Have they gone? I thought to myself. As soon as Aaron and Luke left the car, I got out of the trunk and proceeded to position myself in the back seat and hide in a corner. *What were those gunshots?* A million questions were in my head. I unlocked the car door and stumbled out. Dazed and lightheaded, I leaned on the car and puked on the sidewalk. *Ugh. I'm in a horrible shape.*

I looked around in a daze. There was a store near me, and all the windows were destroyed, glass shards all over the sidewalk. There were aisles turned over in the shop, but that was the least of my worries. *Where am I? Do I still have my phone? How did I get here? Most of all though, where's Ron?*

Still in a daze, I slowly walked away from the gas station. I heard the familiar noise of a police siren. A police car showed up, and the man stepped out and ran towards me. "Hey, are you OK?" He helped me walk to his car, and he talked on his radio away from me, probably calling more officers to this crime scene.

Meanwhile, I looked around. Whatever happened here, Luke and Aaron fought somebody. Ron? No, couldn't be. There were too many gunshots, and I don't think Ron has a gun. Although he might. So, where did those guys go? *They probably went to the forest*, I thought, looking at the forest. Bushes and branches were pushed apart, forming a little gap where anyone can fit through. *They were probably desperate.*

The officer walked up to me. "Alright, I'm going to record your statement about whatever that happened here until the other officers arrive at this scene," he said, whipping up a small notepad. "Let's start off with your name."

"Mary."

"Surname?"

"Smith."

"And what exactly happened here?"

I took a deep breath, and then launched into my story. I was stressed at the Grand Azure Hotel because I already knew that Luke and Aaron would come for my money. I explained how Ron had been captured by them and escaped with his dog, Billy. They both phoned me about what was coming next. I told the officer how we both thought that Luke and Aaron were part of the drug business.

"Luke and Aaron, huh."

I nodded my head and resumed my story. I was stressed out and looking out the window in deep thought. I was worried about Ron and Billy. I was worried about what would come next.

My thoughts were interrupted by loud knocking on the door. I swiveled my head to the door, breaking a sweat. Could it be?

I grabbed a steel pan and quietly stepped to the door. I strained my ears and tried hearing for something on the other side of the door, but all I could hear was my friend's laughter. I eased up, but my right hand still held the steel pan.

I looked through the peephole and saw my friends outside. I felt a wave of relief wash over me which I had never felt before.

I opened the door and smiled. They were laughing and chatting, but one of my friends noticed the steel pan.

"Hey, Mary, is that steel pan for-"

"Yes, Ruby, I know. What happened? Why are you guys here?" I said, throwing my pan on my bed.

"We're going down to the bar! You want to join?" said another one of my friends, Margaret.

"But shouldn't I stay up here?"

"No, it's safe down there too! I'm not joking. They have a bunch of security guards and whatnot, straight from a movie. It'll be fine, trust me."

I sighed and said, "Alright, I'm coming." My friends said they'll be waiting down at the bar. I wore some casual clothes, just normal jeans and a T-shirt. I opened my door and went in the elevator, pressing Floor 1.

Finally, after what seemed like an eternity, I made it down and saw my friends. They waved me over. Then I saw what Margaret had meant about the amount of security being like it was from a movie.

Four guards were standing outside at the doors, patting down everyone before they entered. I even saw "normal" men sitting down and chatting at the bar, but I could tell the outline of a gun at his pocket. They occasionally looked at me, probably making sure I was alright and not hurt.

I walked up to my friends. We started talking and laughing and just having an overall distracted and good time. I completely forgot about Ron, Luke, and Aaron. We had a couple of shots before I got excused and went to the bathroom.

After all those drinks, I was drunk and completely vulnerable. I had no idea I was still in grave danger. I went to the toilet and gagged. Too many drinks made me puke.

I walked out of the stall, wiping my mouth with some paper towels. I spit over in the sink and watched my drunk self in the mirror.

And that's when I saw it. Two men behind me. I looked at them. They looked vaguely familiar. "Luke? Aaron..."

As soon as I said that Aaron shot towards me and choked me. I gagged but couldn't make much noise. "Help..." I said faintly.

"Now, you understand. Do anything, we will not hesitate to kill you. Nobody's going to help you." Aaron whispered in my ear.

Luke chuckled. "Listen, we're janitors now! New job." He pointed at his name tag. The name said something completely different.

I gasped for air, but no sound came out. No air filled my lungs. Suddenly, I felt very exhausted. Is it because I was drunk?

My legs gave out, but Aaron's hard grip on my neck didn't let me fall. I felt my body giving out with no oxygen whatsoever. My eyes started dimming, and I passed out.

The officer nodded. "And you don't remember anything after that? Anything at all?"

"Sorry." I looked down. "I don't."

"That's completely fine. Not to worry. So, we must find someone called Luke and Aaron." He nodded. "Say, there is a drug lord somewhere around here. My entire office has been trying to capture him since he started. I think his name is Santiago or something."

I looked up. "Santiago?"

"Yeah, that's pretty much the only drug lord I've heard of. Luke and Aaron might be working for him if you say, they were part of the drug business."

"I never said it was true. It's just the most reasonable explanation for all the guns and money. Plus, Luke and Aaron have been fighting someone." I waved at the destroyed store. "Those people probably had a lot of firepower. Guns and grenades."

"Hmm, alright. Thanks for the information. We'll be looking for DNA samples while we are out here." He pointed to the forensics team. There was police tape around the area, so no one could come inside. A crowd had formed around the tape, and the press was there too. "You're going to the hospital next. Standard procedure."

"But what about the drug lord you mentioned? And Luke and Aaron? What are you going to do about them?"

He looked at the forensics team. "They'll figure out who's been here. Plus, we could already tell someone ran into the forest." He pointed to the gap between the bushes. "Listen, it'll be alright. You just need to stay put for a day, and when you're fine, we'll release you and you can go and do whatever you want to do."

I nodded and walked into the police car. I saw the officer go to his lieutenant and say something which wasn't audible from where I was. He walked back to his car and started the engine. "The hospital's not far," he said.

I nodded and laid back. With the police, I think I'm safe. For now. Plus, where was Ron when Luke and Aaron kidnapped me? He wasn't there yet?

"Hey, officer, do you have a cell phone?" I asked.

He nodded and gave me his phone through the bars. "Call whoever you want, just make sure to give me it back, once we're at the hospital."

I nodded, dialing Ron's number. He didn't pick up. I dialed his number again, worrying. This time, I heard his voice.

"Hello, who is this..." His voice was quiet and hollow, like he had been crying.

"Ron?" I started.

I didn't hear a response for a good fifteen seconds. "M-Mary?" His voice was louder now.

"Ron!"

"Mary! Oh my god, oh my god! Mary, are you alright?" I heard sirens.

I heard loud panting, and I heard the familiar sound of a dog giving a bark. "Billy!" I smiled, remembering him. "I haven't seen you in a long time!"

Billy barked again.

"Ron, are you in an ambulance?"

"Yes, I am. I'm going to get my leg treated." He sounded relieved.

"Oh Ron, you wouldn't believe what happened! I was kidnapped, and then I heard gunshots and shouting. A kind officer picked me up and now is driving me to the hospital."

"Thank God! Are you fine?"

"Yes, I'm alright. It's just... I haven't met you in a long time," I said, tears welling up in my eyes.

"Same here. Just come back to me safe, okay? Meet you at the hospital. Bye."

"Bye."

With that, he hung up.

I tapped the officer's shoulder and gave the phone back to him, again wondering what would come next.

I groaned and laid on my back at the bottom of the cliff. Where was Luke? I knew we would get separated!

I craned my neck to look at my body. It did not look good at all.

There were some nasty scratches, and my ripped t-shirt was covered in my blood. There was so much pain, it made my head dizzy. The pain was hell, like someone had lit my body on fire and left me there to die.

I couldn't move, so I turned my head to look around. There was a pond nearby. I could wash up there. I had to take off my shirt too. It was reeking, and I had no idea, since how long I had been lying down in the forest. I knew I was lost, and Luke was probably lost too.

I yelped, as I tried moving my arms. Groaning loudly in pain, I pushed myself to the pond, still lying down.

There was a tree root in the way, and as I crawled over it, it bent my back, and I heard a crack. "Ah! Ouch, ouch, ouch."

I finally crawled over it, but didn't feel any sense of relief. All I thought was that the pain had gone.

I was just a foot away from the pond at this point. Just a little more.

After what seemed like an eternity but was really just five seconds, I splashed onto the pond, floating carelessly. The pain still hadn't gone, but I saw blood getting washed off. I smiled to myself.

The cold water woke me up. It also felt good after the humid temperatures in the forest had made me sweaty. Once I started to think properly, I looked at the river we had fallen into. I was in the "pond" created by the waterfall there. There were light waves crashing against me because of the waterfall. I would have to climb back up there, if I had any chance of escaping. I had no idea how deep and thick this forest was.

I looked around for any signs of Luke but didn't find him anywhere. *Ugh, we really are separated. That stupid man didn't realize, falling off a waterfall could've killed us!* But I couldn't help but wonder, how he had saved us with the stupidest plan in humanity.

I was still afloat, thinking. All those thoughts had distracted me from the pain, and now when I wasn't thinking, the pain washed over me.

I winced and turned over to float on my stomach. The water had a little tint of red, but fortunately, it was hard to notice. I opened my eyes in the water and looked down. It was dark down there, and nothing new except little fish swimming about.

I turned over on my back again and swam to the shore with resting backstroke. The little waves made by the waterfall washed me up to the shore. I tried standing up, to failure. I tried again, and this time, I tripped and fell back into the water. I tried again, and this time, I almost fell but regained my balance, finally standing up.

I stood there, shaking my head vigorously to get water off my hair. *Now what?* I could tell my legs were literally going to die, if I even took one step. My mind told me to just stand there and get used to it, but part of me told me to go and find Luke.

I took one step, and like I predicted, hell broke through in my leg. I winced and exhaled, taking another step. My right leg wasn't as bad as my left for some reason, so when I took steps, I put more weight on my right than my left leg.

I inwardly screamed as I almost tripped over, giving my weight to my left leg. I quickly shifted weight to my right leg. I looked up into the woods. *You know what? It'll be better if Luke comes here. It'll be easier for him to find me.*

And so, I sat down. All those steps for nothing. Not like I really went far. I was a good five feet away from the pond. But that was a sort of an achievement for me.

Ugh! All these useless thoughts! Am I going crazy or what? I touched my head and didn't feel blood thankfully. Why was I surprised?

I heard rustling behind me, and I whipped my head behind. Luke!

"Hey! Aaron..." Luke seemed to be in a worse shape than me. He turned around faced upwards. I crawled towards him.

"Oh! What happened?" I spoke.

"I got shot. Near my stomach." He said each word slowly as if, weighing what he had to say.

"Hmm. Alright. Well, we're screwed. We're going to become animals or something, learn to fish and hunt. This isn't any Cast Away," I grumbled. "You're shot and we both can't walk." I sighed. "Now what?"

"No idea." He sighed and winced. I looked at him. "Seriously? So, we have no hope of getting out of here."

"Pretty much." He stared at the cloudless sky absentmindedly.

Frustration boiled inside me. "How can you be so calm! We're stranded in the middle of nowhere, with nowhere to go, our only hope of escape is climbing an unclimbable cliff, with our stupid ragged legs, and most of all, we can't move, means that we can't hunt, fish, or do anything!"

"I mean, we have berries." He waved all around us. "This is the forest after all."

"But we have no idea if they are poisonous or not. We'll die out here."

"Don't say that yet."

I turned to him, angry now. "Be REAL, Luke! We can't treat this crap!" I pointed to my legs. "We cannot escape, Luke! It's literally impossible!"

"Nothing is."

I looked at Luke in disbelief. Seriously?

"No harm in trying to scale the cliff, right? We haven't even tried yet."

I looked at the cliff. It wasn't that big, and it wasn't straight up. I could easily do it with my healthy legs. I could even sprint up the cliff with them. But with these dirty, bleeding legs, I can't do anything.

"Listen. Let's sleep for a night here, then wake up and see if we can walk. We should be able to walk then, right? I mean, worth a try. Plus, there are trees up there, so we can take breaks."

"Easier said than done."

"Look, the sun's already setting. Let's get some rest. After all, we need to sleep."

As soon as I heard the word sleep, my eyes started drooping like they had just remembered what sleeping was. "Yeah, sure. Sleep sounds like a good idea to me."

And just like that, I laid back, closed my eyes, and drifted off to a deep sleep.

Chapter - 12
Trail

When I dropped her off at the hospital, I immediately turned back to go back to the crime scene.

It was a hot day out there, and on the ride here, she had told me that she was stuck in Luke and Aaron's trunk. She had explained how when some random men she never met or knew opened the trunk for her, she had crawled over the back seat and hid in a corner. Right after that, she heard shouting and gunshots. Then she had heard the rustling of bushes and then it was quiet, so she stepped out of the car.

That was the story. Good thing I got a recording of it, even though I won't be forgetting it.

As I arrived at the crime scene, I showed my ID to the officer outside of the police tape and entered the scene. There was blood too, and I saw a couple of people talking near the blood and pointing in different directions.

I walked up to my lieutenant.

"Hey Silas. You were the one who took her statement, right? And dropped her off to the hospital? What was her name?"

"Mary Smith. She's the wife of Ron Smith and they have a dog named Billy."

"What did she say?"

"About some people named Luke and Aaron trying to rob her of "their" money."

I started explaining how Luke and Aaron were two of her clients in her business and they had given her money to grow. Mary used it, but then she messed up and crashed the business, leaving people without jobs and Luke and Aaron without money. So now they want that sum of money back.

"Sounds stupid that they would go through all this," he said, waving at the store.

"Yeah, but the thing is, Luke and Aaron are probably part of the drug business, so they probably stole the money from their drug lord and gave it to Mary."

"Wait, but how exactly would they steal it? And if it's Santiago we're talking about, he would track them down."

"Exactly. Even I thought it was Santiago. It all fits. Luke and Aaron probably are dead by now." I looked at the gap between the bushes. "Or they ran for their lives into the woods."

"So, are you suggesting we send a search party to arrest them and put them on trial?"

"Probably if we want to get anywhere with this case."

"Hmm. Alright. Nice thinking, Silas. I'll see if we can send a search party. You go with BPA and check out what they're doing."

I nodded. I never liked our BPA team. They enjoy analyzing blood patterns. Either they're used to it, or they're just a bunch of weirdos or psychos.

I walked up towards them. "Hey guys, what's happening?"

One guy stood up to talk to me. "Oh, hey Silas. We were just looking at which direction they were running. It seems like one guy was crushed under the weight of an aisle, and then as soon as that happened, our suspects, Luke and Aaron, ran up to the window and jumped, giving them some scratches. Here, let me show you."

He pointed to the window. "This is definitely not a window broken by a gunshot. This window is completely shattered." He pointed to the shards of glass all over the sidewalk. "See the blood? We tested it to be a guy named Luke." He raised his eyebrows. "Our suspect."

"Nice work. So, you're saying that the drug lord's men came here to get Mary's money instead of helping Luke and Aaron?"

"Drug lord? Aaron? Mary?"

I filled in on him the information we had so far with the interrogation with Mary.

"Hmm. Yes, probably. There are other blood samples there too, like someone from Santi's team jumped too, to chase Luke and Aaron."

"Who is it?"

"Some guy named Leonardo Hernandez. Anyways, what happened next is more shocking. There's a teeny tiny trail of blood leading to the gap in the bushes. It tested as Aaron's." He looked at me. "I think we should send a search party down there, so they follow the trail of blood."

"Hmm, alright. I already spoke to the lieutenant about search parties. He'll probably send one."

"Alright. Well, I'll go back to work."

I never knew BPA was useful. Or maybe I just hadn't seen them work before.

I walked back to my lieutenant. "Those guys are working hard."

"Good to hear. You're excused for your hard work. You can go and do whatever you want."

"Thank you."

And with that, I headed back to my car, hopefully to chill at home and watch T.V. Hopefully no more crime scenes.

All I can say is that it worked. My plan worked!

We had scaled the cliff, and we had to take two breaks, but it still worked! Worth it.

As soon as me and Aaron went up, we saw a little trail of blood. Hard to notice, but I pointed it out. This was bad. This little trail of blood was all the police needed to solve this case.

"If they take a DNA test on this, we're done for!" I said, looking at the blood. "Hey, what are you doing?" I looked at Aaron, kicking dirt around.

"Covering our blood," he said.

"They already took a sample of it. It's obvious. We'll go outside right now and see the crime scene. Some random people probably called the police after hearing the gun shots. But the real question is, how did Mary escape? She probably leaked everything! We're so-"

"Shut up." Aaron said, following the line of blood. "If they did a crime scene, then we need to get the heck out of here. We need a car. And now, Santiago's against us, so I guess no car. And we can't do anything about that. If Santi's against us, that means he will kill us no matter what." He turned to me. "Meaning, the only way to survive, is go to Europe or something, which isn't possible, now that the police want us to be arrested, or kill Santiago, which isn't possible either."

Aaron continued walking and I followed in complete silence. No car, no transportation. No transportation means Santiago would keep following us until we're cornered and dead. Should we team up with the police then? They'd probably arrest us then and there, but is it worth a try? If they help, Santi could go behind bars, but if they don't, our safest option is probably to be behind bars.

"Hey, Aaron. Stop." Aaron stopped and looked at me. "What is it?" he asked.

"Look, I've been thinking of a plan. How to avoid, you know, dying."

"Alright, I'm listening."

"Ok. We must talk to the police." I stopped Aaron as he opened his mouth to talk, his expression frustrated. "No, no, listen! Don't talk." I said my next words carefully. "Our safest bet is to talk to the police. If they help us in fighting Santi, I know he won't die, but he will be behind bars for a long time, probably going to a high-level security prison, God knows where. But if the police refuses and arrests us, it IS safer than walking the streets with Santi on our tail. Santiago won't be able to catch us, if we're in jail."

"Do you know how many years; we'll spend in jail? Probably fifty! In fifty years, I'll be around eighty! I probably won't even survive until we will get out of jail! Same goes for you. We have broken the law, tons of times for working for Santiago, kidnapping Mary, Ron, and some random dog, and even shooting people!"

"So, you're saying dying is better than staying in jail for fifty years?"

That shut him up.

"It's our best way out. That's for sure."

He seemed to consider for a moment. He groaned. "Fine."

I nodded my head in triumph, and we resumed following the blood trail.

As soon as we stepped out, I bumped into a police tape. "Uh oh," I whispered, creeping back into the woods.

Aaron looked at me and hissed, "Come back here! This was your plan after all, right?"

"But I didn't mean now! What if the lieutenant isn't here? Or the captain? I plan on talking to the lieutenant though, since she's probably in charge of this case."

"Fine by me. Let's wait it out then. Move left until you feel like they won't see us in this 'trail' and wait."

I nodded and pushed vines out of the way and tried to avoid rustling. I winced as a spike on the vine, cut me.

"Try not to get hurt more," I warned Aaron. He nodded. "We don't want the legs getting that beat up again."

After a minute, we felt safe and we crouched down, pushing away vines carefully and avoiding the spikes on them. This forest is infested with these things, and I could only wish, I had a knife. My stomach was still aching like hell. Good thing Aaron was helping me walk.

We both also had tons of bug bites, and pretty much my entire body was begging to be scratched. I've probably already gotten infected with the wounds from the gun and the cuts.

I slowly got comfortable to avoid rustling, and I told Aaron to do so too.

We waited for a good hour, and it looked like it was noon already.

"Aaron, let's move. They should have gone now." He nodded and we slowly stood up and started walking back to the trail. We took a left and saw that the police tape was still there. "Wait," I said. "They're still here?"

"Probably not. They may just want no one to get to this crime scene." I nodded my head. That was probably the plan.

After Aaron held to help me to get in the car, we creeped up out of the woods and walked out. There was nobody there. We saw our car, still parked in the parking lot. I went under the police tape and stepped inside

"Where are the keys?" Aaron said.

"No idea." I said, looking around. It was probably in the evidence bags, or?

I checked my pockets. I remembered driving there and grabbing the keys to get inside the store, so where else could it be?

I heard the familiar jingle of the keys.

"Ta-da! Found it!" I said in a sing-song voice. We walked toward the car, Aaron easing me down in the back seat and going to drive.

"Where to?" I asked Aaron. He seemed to ponder for a bit. "The hospital. They should take care of us. I'll go to the nearest hospital. After we get treated, we're going to straight to the police station, alright?"

He stepped on the pedal, going straight for the hospital. I could only hope they would treat it and be nice, but at the same time, the police might show up to question us while we're still patients. And I'll have to get the bullet surgically removed.

This was going to be a long day.

"Any update on Luke and Aaron? As well as Mary?" I said, frustrated.

"No, sir. Not yet. We have no idea where they fell off the waterfall. As for Mary, well, we checked the Grand Azure Hotel, and she wasn't there. We have no idea where she is, sir."

"Are you serious? You guys can't do anything! The police are probably after me now. So annoying..." I put my hand on my head and exhaled. If the police were after me, I would be in danger of getting arrested. Meaning my only way of getting out of this mess is, by going somewhere far from America.

I stood up and left the room. I live in a huge mansion with all my workers, two pools, a golf course, my entire family, a shooting range, and a big garden, I love to spend time in. Of course, I have my office, where I run everything, I need to do, which isn't much, since my workers have taken over.

I walked up the spiral staircase and knocked on my dad's door. "Eh? Who's it?"

"It's me, your son. God damn it, father, how many times will you be drunk?"

He opened the door and let me in. "Listen, father. I have something important to tell you."

"Huh? What is it?" he asked, grabbing his liquor bottle.

I snatched it away from him and gave him a glare. "This is serious." I told him to sit down on his bed, so we could talk.

"Listen, I'm dead serious right now. The police are hunting us down. They'll probably be on us by tomorrow, so we need to be ready. when it happens. Forget Mary. Forget Luke and Aaron. Our family's safety is a priority. We will leave America at 5 sharp tomorrow morning. Don't be drunk, otherwise you won't be able to wake up."

He looked at me with wide eyes, as if not understanding what I said. "Wait, what? This is all too sudden. We're leaving America? And going where?"

"I'm thinking Australia. I have some friends there who might take us in. I also have a small business going around there."

"Australia? That seems out of the blue. And you never mentioned any friends or a small business there."

"Listen, that's not important. We need to pack up now. Grab all the money you can. We'll need it."

"Fine. But what about our business here? This is like our headquarters."

"Oh, father, this isn't a joke! Pack up now!"

"Ok, ok. I just need to have some shut eye for a moment. Be back with you in a sec. Call my servant to pack my stuff up."

"No, I can't! No one needs to know about this except of our pilot and our family." As soon as I said that, I stood up and left abruptly without saying a word.

I then went to my mom's room and told her about it. She was shocked, but she didn't argue. At least she wasn't drunk.

I found all my cousins and brothers and told them about it too. They started packing immediately.

I then went to my pilot and told him to be ready for Australia tomorrow at 5 in the morning and to ask my right-hand man to take care of things while I'm away. Honestly, who knows when would things settle down and I would come back...

But most importantly I needed to fix things before I went. And that would mean finding all the five brats, who ruined everything. They're injured and one's shot. Where else could they be besides the hospital?

I smiled at my thinking. I can finally get revenge for my long-lost money.

Chapter - 13
War

I didn't even have to climb out of the car. The men there took my dog and put me on a stretcher. "Where is he going to go?" They looked at me and replied, "The vet. Then the shelter. Don't worry, you can get him back after your treatment is done." I nodded, and let the men put me on a stretcher and wheeled me to the surgery room. I was finally being operated. Thank God. The throbbing pain disturbed me for a while, and it still did, but I didn't really notice it with all the worry and stress.

Now, I noticed the pain. It was like my entire leg had been dipped in oil and then put in a raging fire. My entire thigh throbbed with pain, and I groaned loudly in pain. The pain was also affecting my shin, although I had been shot in the thigh. *Damn it! This thing hurts! How the hell was I even surviving for this long?!*

The men quickly led me to a room, where I guessed, I would get examined. My thigh was now vibrating a little in pain, but the doctor held it firmly and told the other doctor to deliver anesthesia for the surgery. *Oh crap!*

The other doctor walked up towards me and grabbed a mask lowering it down on my face. I took a deep breath in, preparing to hold my breath, but the doctor stopped.

"Not to worry, it's just going to make you sleep." I hesitated, but I exhaled. He then put on the mask.

For a second, nothing happened. But as soon as I took a breath in, it was like my entire body was slightly relieved in pain. I took another breath, and my body relaxed, my eyes dimming. Within seconds, I was asleep.

"We need to be quiet." I was telling my men what to do once we were at the hospital. "Any sign of Ron, Mary, Luke, Aaron, or even the dog, kill them. I don't care about my money anymore; I just want them dead. Understand?" The men nodded their heads. "Go get some handguns. We need to be quiet when we enter. Nobody should notice a thing." They nodded again and jogged off to get their guns.

I sighed and grabbed an extra magazine and a handgun as well. I told everyone to wear thick pants so that the outline of the gun in your pocket is not visible. Hopefully it works.

I hugged my mom and dad and said bye to my family, then I walked to an SUV, pulling on my jacket. I told the men to get two different SUV's and split up, so we look as innocent as possible, not until we get the brats, who stole my money.

I sat down comfortably in the car. There was just me and another guy in this car. We didn't want it packed. Four people meeting a person wouldn't be so subtle. We had also grabbed silencers to ensure a hopefully quiet death. I won't just leave these people alone.

"Drive," I said to the other man. He nodded.

The other SUV was scheduled to leave five minutes later. I checked the time. One minute had passed since we started. If all this goes right, another SUV would come in as soon as, we called it. This time, it was packed and ready to fight, just in case acting innocent doesn't cut it. It was like our emergency SUV.

We were here. It was only a 5-minute drive to this hospital. Plus, I had a feeling they would be right here. Or at least Luke and Aaron would be. If Ron and Mary aren't, it's OK. My right-hand man will get him tomorrow while I'm on the plane to Australia.

I stepped out of the car, telling my man to step out too. If Luke and Aaron would be anywhere, it was here. One of my men had shot Luke after all.

There was an ambulance in front of the hospital. The man on the stretcher was groaning loudly, obviously in pain. I was able to see his face. He looked like-

"Luke," I whispered under my breath. I nudged my man. He was looking at something else. "Aaron," I said loudly. He too was there, injured. But Aaron wasn't in pain with his eyes closed. He was looking straight at me.

I quickly averted my eyes, but I knew he had seen me. *Crap! My entire plan could easily go in ruins with this one incident. He needs to die right now before he escapes!*

I signaled to the man to move in. He nodded, and we both jogged to the hospital. We climbed the stairs and stuck our heads in, looking around, but Luke was nowhere to be found. We then went up to the person at the front desk, but there was a line.

"3 people. God damn it. Fricking line."

My man stood there, obviously impatient. I made sure to pick a man who remembered Luke and Aaron and how they looked like. I also made sure to pick one, who had a grudge against them, and it looks like I picked the right one.

I looked at my watch. Any minute now, and my men would pull up to the parking lot and get over here. *Damn it! This is not supposed to happen!*

I looked at the man I was with. I didn't even know his name. I told him to go outside and call the other SUV to not get out here and wait for our call. He nodded and went outside, leaving me alone. *What now? What will happen?* I glanced nervously at the sheriff on guard duty. *If anything goes wrong, this man can arrest me. Then I won't be going to Australia. I would be caught up rotting in a cell. And then what happens to my family?*

I shook my head, trying to shake off the negative thoughts. The line was taking a long time. I had to do something, or otherwise it would be too late.

When it was finally my turn, I was practically fuming. "Hello sir, how can I help you?"

I put on a fake smile. "Hello. I need to visit an old friend."

"And what is that friend's name?"

"Luke." I coughed. "Uh... Luke Shepherd."

"Stay right here. I'll be with you in a moment." She walked out of the front desk and straight to the sheriff. *What the…?!*

I ran.

I ran for my life. Something fishy was going on around here. Did Luke or Aaron already tell the police and warn them? Crap.

I bolted for the nearest hallway, knowing Luke or Aaron were in one of those doors. "HOLD IT!" I heard the sheriff shout. Oh god. This was taking an ugly turn.

I pulled out my phone and dialed the emergency SUV. It picked up immediately. "Need help, sir?"

"GET THE HELL OUT HERE! NOW!!!" I disconnected before he could argue or say a word. Still running, I dialed the man's number I came here with. As soon as he picked up, I heard myself say, "GET BACK INSIDE!" As I did with the emergency SUV, I disconnected immediately, having trust in my men, that they would get over here to help.

"I WILL SHOOT!" The officer warned me, probably pulling out his gun. I took a quick left and busted inside the nearest door there. I held my breath, slamming the door shut.

I heard the policeman skid to a stop, also opening the door to the room I was in. I was hiding behind the door, so as soon as he would open it, I would shoot.

As planned, I shot the door when it opened, hoping that it would hit its target. I heard a groan. *Yes! I hit him!*

I then jumped out of my hiding spot and tried grabbing the sheriff, but instead, I felt myself getting pushed back. *What the! I don't see a gunshot wound! He faked the wound!*

At any moment now, more police would come.

He pushed me back to a drawer, knocking my breath out as I hit it. Determined, the policeman pulled out his taser and tried shooting me with it, but I was too quick. I grabbed his hand, and with his aim somewhere else, he shot it accidentally. As soon as I heard the taser go off, I slapped his hand away and the taser went flying away from his grasp. I tried to kick his balls, but he backed off and elbowed me on the ribs. I groaned, but I didn't lose composure. I punched him in the stomach, and he winced in pain and backed off, giving me enough time to get him.

I ran up to him, preparing to kick him, but I saw a familiar face. *It's the guy I came here with!*

Sure enough, it was the man I had come here with, I had no idea what his name was.

He grabbed the man and put him in a headlock, choking him hard. The man soon fell, unconscious, to the ground.

Me and the man wasted no time. We heard sirens already outside and men shouting, telling everyone to evacuate. *Crap! We're cornered!*

But I knew my men were coming. I heard guns outside, even the automatic kind. I heard shouting and literally just chaos. *Crap! If I knew all this would've happened, I would've never done this!*

But I knew there was no turning back. I pulled out my gun and went back, grabbing a doctor by his arm and shouting, "WHERE THE HELL ARE LUKE AND AARON?!"

"Uh, uh, please! Don't hurt me!"

"JUST TELL ME!!!" "Over there! Over there!" He pointed at the door, to the end of the hallway. I dashed to it, and busted in, but didn't see him. *He escaped? Or was the doctor lying...*

I peeked out to see Luke in crutches, wobbling away as fast as he can. He opened another door and waved at something, that something probably being Aaron. I growled. Those men won't be going far.

I raised my gun to shoot them, and my man raised his gun too. We both shot and ran to them, but we missed. When we were just about to shoot the second one, they disappeared at a turn. I still shot, but I broke into a sprint, knowing they would hide somewhere. I had to get there quick.

I looked behind and saw my friend fighting against 3 police officers. He was overwhelmed easily, and I wanted to help him, but I had to run away. More officers were coming up, and I still had to find Luke and Aaron.

I sprinted at top speed to Aaron and Luke. Those guys were as good as dead. I saw them drop their crutches and run for their lives, sprinting and limping and the same time. I pulled out my gun and aimed-

I felt a man grab me on the shoulders and kick my spine with his knee. I coughed out spit, giving that man enough time to – wait – bite me on the leg?

War

I felt jaws close on my leg and heard myself howl in pain. The pain quickly spread throughout my leg. I felt a warm liquid trickling down my leg and realized it was my own blood. What the hell was even biting me?

I put every ounce of my strength into pushing the man back. As soon as I felt the man get pushed back, I tried spinning to face him but stopped when the thing biting my leg didn't go away. I looked down, and there was a literal rottweiler biting my leg.

Was it rabid? I pointed my gun at him but saw the man running towards me in desperation. His dog?

The dog released his grip and jumped to bite whatever the hell he was after next, so I elbowed him away, leaving him on the floor whining.

I got taken by surprise when the man jumped at me, punching my face with his right arm. I went flying to the right, stopping my fall only by the hospital's wall. I wiped my face with one hand, looking at my blood-stained sleeve. *God damn it! I need help!*

The dog stood up and pounced at me, growling loudly. I pointed my gun at it, but the man slapped it away. *No!*

The dog bit my leg again, and I howled in pain again. I felt my blood trickling down again. I can't lose!

I punched the man with all my might. He stumbled backwards and fell on his knees. I tried kicking him with my knee, but that heavy rottweiler pounced on me, growling at the top of its lungs. I kicked him away, and he fell whining in pain.

I turned around and tried looking for my gun. It didn't really go flying far, but it wasn't there. I looked up and saw Aaron pointing the gun at me, Luke sitting down, exhausted.

"You go get out of here. I don't want to see your face here again. And if I do, I won't hesitate to shoot," he said. He sounded exhausted and in pain. After all, he was still a cornered rat. Gun or not, I could still beat the living crap out of him, using the man I fought as a shield.

I grinned at my quick thinking. "Really? You're going to shoot me? Good luck with that. Do you know what'll happen to you if you kill me somehow?" I chuckled. "I took you under my wing. I trusted you with my money. And yet you stole it. I mean, who's at the wrong here?"

Aaron seemed to hesitate. "I know I did wrong when that happened. But what's happened recently, I think you should forget it. It's your life or your money. Can't really enjoy money when you're dead, don't you think?"

I growled, anger boiling inside me. Only if I had a gun. This little rat was mocking at me with my gun. He stole my money. I'm only trying to get it back.

"Why the hell would you steal from a drug lord, that's my question. You're insane." I laughed. "Jesus, man, I really thought that you were a wimp. Guess I'm sadly mistaken." In one quick and fluid motion, I grabbed the man who fought with me earlier. "Not like you can shoot me now, can you? Your big heart doesn't want to kill people. I know you would never kill me. Stalemate."

He looked at me and smiled. "You really think I won't kill you? Man, are you wrong?" He pointed the gun straight at my face. I slowly went behind the man, so that he can't shoot at my face.

I suddenly charged, using the man's unconscious body to my advantage. Aaron stepped back a little, surprised, but stood his ground. He tried looking for options, but you can't really do anything, when you can't shoot the man, you want to shoot.

And that's when I fell. The same searing pain jolted my body upright, and I lost balance, falling. Did he shoot me somehow? Luke couldn't reach me. He was very weak after the surgery.

I heard growling and barking behind me. The dog. He was biting my back now instead of my leg.

I turned around to stop him, but Aaron took advantage and grabbed my arms. *No! I'm losing!*

The man stepped up to me, looking at Aaron and Luke with deep hatred. If he hated them, why was he against me?

"Billy, stop." The dog growled in my face and stepped back to his owner.

I was twisting and turning in pain, groaning loudly. It was literal hell. But I was helpless. A dog bit me three times, I got beat up by a man and two other men put me at gunpoint to help, when I beat up the dog and the man. I inwardly smiled. It took a dog and three men to beat me. Not bad.

"Look. I think you are Ron." I pointed at the dog's owner. "Listen, these people Luke and Aaron kidnapped your entire family including you for my money. They stole my money. They are in the wrong here."

Ron looked at Luke and Aaron. "You told them to, didn't you?"

"Well yes, because it's MY MONEY! These men STOLE IT! Why the hell are you against me? It makes no sense! I never even met you before this."

Ron looked at me. "I'll deal with them later." He looked at them. "We still must sort things out. But you are going to prison. Now, I don't know about Luke and Aaron, but really, I want them to go to prison with you. See what happens to you guys behind bars. All of you had ruined my past week. Luke and Aaron stole your money and gave it to Mary. Mary failed to use it properly, so she went on vacation to deal with her stress. Meanwhile, you gave Luke and Aaron a second chance to get that money back and give it to you. But I mean, I've heard stories about you. You really weren't just going to let them go, am I right?"

Damn. He was smart.

"So, what were these guys supposed to do under some serious peer pressure? I don't know. They don't have a lot of money, honestly. I seriously despise them, but honestly, I understand their decisions. Although all of you are at fault." He stood up. "I'll talk with the police. Meanwhile, you guys just keep him down. Billy, come on."

War

I was hurt. My entire body was in pain, but when Ron told me to leave, I dutifully followed.

He went outside and I followed. It sure was a sight to see. There were men getting arrested and police everywhere. Those men were outnumbered from the start.

Ron walked up to a policeman and said something about Santiago, Luke and Aaron. The police man nodded and said that he'll talk to his lieutenant. He said that we can go back home. A feeling of relief washed over me. We can go home. We didn't have to worry about getting kidnapped, worry about a family member dying, worry about what comes next.

At home, you don't have to worry about anything.

I saw a car pull up and a policeman driving the car. Mary got out of the car and the policeman walked her over to us.

"Ron! You look beaten up! What happened?" Mary questioned, looking at Ron.

"I'm fine, as long as you're here," Ron said grinning. "Billy and I took down Santiago. I don't know what to do with Luke and Aaron, but they helped with getting Santiago arrested." Mary smiled at him.

"Looks like you've been working a lot, eh? And you too Billy!" She crouched down and kissed my face. She looked up at Ron. "Why is his mouth covered in blood? Don't tell me..."

Ron smiled. "Yeah. That's what I meant by helping." He too crouched down and rubbed my ears.

"Ron, you still need to go to the hospital. The surgery might be done, but looking at these injuries, you might need to go again. Same goes for you, Billy." All I want to do now is to go home.

"Nah. We both just need to get checked up, no worries. After all, we didn't get shot or anything serious."

Mary sighed. "Fine, do whatever you want. But I bet you both also want to go home, because I sure do."

They both got up, and Ron grabbed my leash. We told a police officer that we were leaving, and they said that we could as long as we go to the station after we rest. We nodded, just wanting to get out of here.

The car ride home was like a dream come true. My anticipation for stretching and lazing around in my dog bed skyrocketed when we climbed out of the car. I could tell everyone was looking forward to going home. And I could tell, I was going to take a long bath.

When we opened the door, the familiar smell of our home greeted us with welcoming hands. Ron took off my leash and Mary went inside the shower immediately. "Home sweet home," Ron whispered.

After my shower, I lazed on my dog bed. I never really gave a second thought about where I slept or how I did. I grabbed my chew toy and went to sleep as soon as I hit the bed.

When I woke up, I stretched my muscles and walked out of the room. Mary and Ron were sitting on the couch, munching on chips and watching a movie. I went to the water bowl and drank my water after a long time, then sat with Ron, so that he could give me a snack.

Still eating, Mary spoke up. "You know what? We should celebrate!"

Ron grinned. "Sure! What food should we buy first? And should we call the neighbors over? They seem to love parties."

"Oh no, it's just going to be the three of us." Mary kissed Ron's cheek and reached down to kiss my head. "Let's buy. hmm... pizza!"

I looked at Ron. Ron was looking at me with a smile, wide-eyed. Pizza tastes good, but I guess it's kind of cursed.

www.ingramcontent.com/pod-product-compliance
Lightning Source LLC
LaVergne TN
LVHW061557070526
838199LV00077B/7090